STAR WARS
EPISODE III
REVENGE OF THE SITH

TITAN
BOOKS

The events in this story
take place nineteen years
before *Star Wars: A New Hope*

EPISODE III
REVENGE OF THE SITH

Based on the story and screenplay by
George Lucas

Adapted by
Miles Lane

Art by
Doug Wheatley

Coloring by
Christopher Chuckry

Page 2 and 5 illustrations by
Dave Dorman

lettering by
Michael David Thomas

publisher
Mike Richardson

collection designer
Keith Wood

associate editor
Jeremy Barlow

editor
Randy Stradley

special thanks to
Sue Rostoni and Amy Gary
at Lucas Licensing

STAR WARS: EPISODE III – REVENGE OF THE SITH™

Published by
Titan Books
a division of Titan Publishing Group Ltd.
144 Southwark Street
London
SE1 0UP

What did you think of this book?
We love to hear from our readers.
Please email us at:
readerfeedback@titanemail.com, or
write to us at the above address.

www.titanbooks.com
www.starwars.com

First edition: May 2005
ISBN: 1-84576-058-1

3 5 7 9 10 8 6 4 2

Printed in Italy

DORMAN

War! The Republic is crumbling under attacks by the Separatist leader, Count Dooku. There are heroes on both sides. Evil is everywhere.

In a stunning move, the fiendish droid leader, General Grievous, has swept into the Republic capital and kidnapped Chancellor Palpatine, leader of the Galactic Senate.

As the Separatist Droid Army attempts to flee the besieged Capital with their valuable hostage, two Jedi Knights lead a desperate mission to rescue the captive Chancellor....

ANAKIN, THEY'RE ALL OVER ME!

MOVE TO THE RIGHT --

-- SO I CAN GET A CLEAR SHOT AT THEM.

LOCK ONTO HIM, ARTOO...

WE GOT HIM!

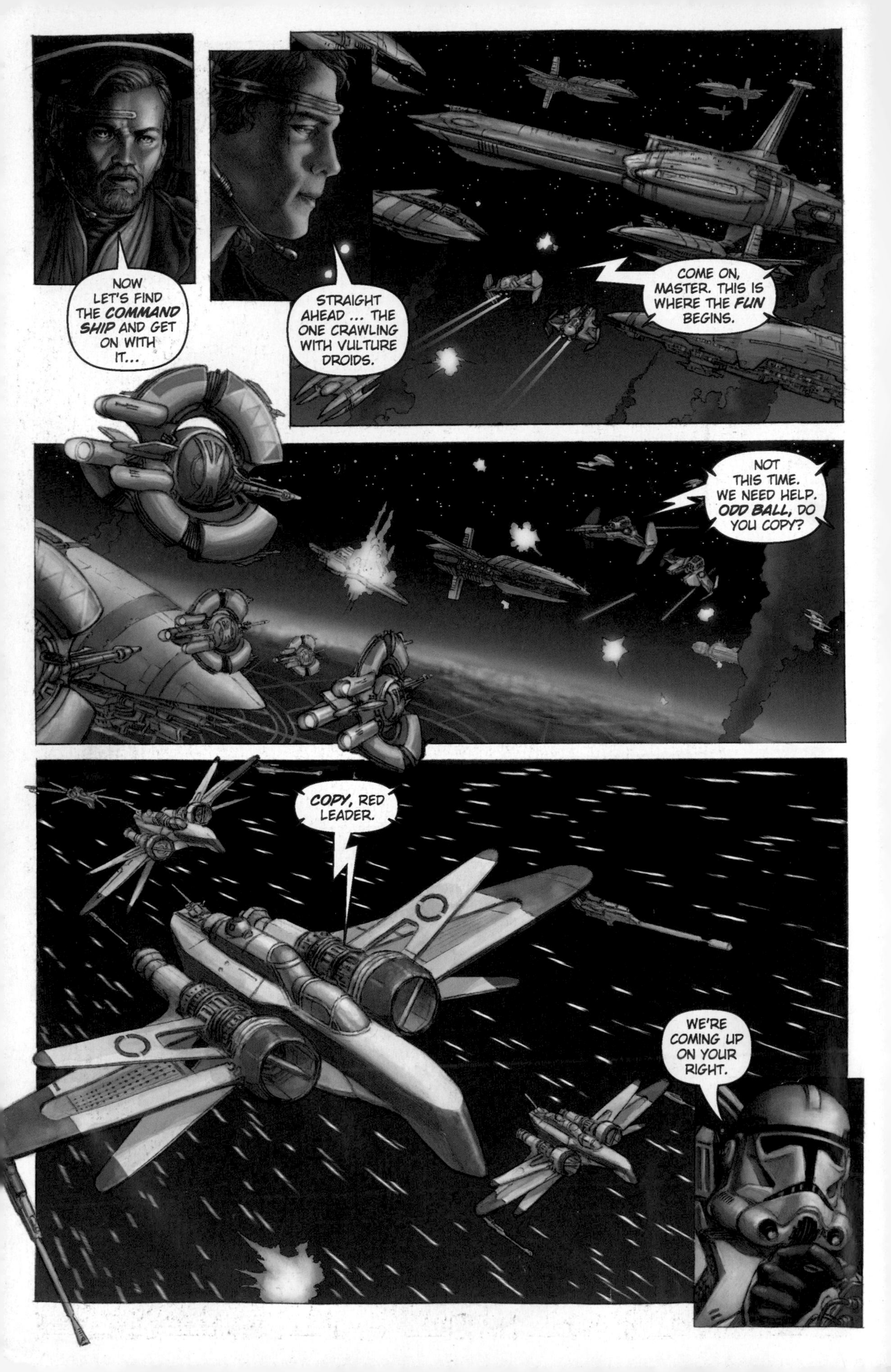
NOW LET'S FIND THE COMMAND SHIP AND GET ON WITH IT...
STRAIGHT AHEAD ... THE ONE CRAWLING WITH VULTURE DROIDS.
COME ON, MASTER. THIS IS WHERE THE FUN BEGINS.
NOT THIS TIME. WE NEED HELP. ODD BALL, DO YOU COPY?
COPY, RED LEADER.
WE'RE COMING UP ON YOUR RIGHT.

THERE ARE TOO MANY OF THEM!
I'M GOING TO HELP THEM OUT!
NO, YOU'RE NOT!
THEY'RE DOING THEIR JOB SO WE CAN DO OURS. HEAD FOR THE COMMAND SHIP!
MISSILES!
I'M HIT!
MASTER -- BUZZ DROIDS!
GET OUT OF HERE, ANAKIN --

-- THERE'S NOTHING YOU CAN DO.
I'M NOT LEAVING YOU, MASTER!
STEADY ... STEADY...
ANAKIN, HOLD YOUR FIRE!
BLAST IT!
MY CONTROLS ARE GONE!
STAY ON MY WING! HEAD FOR THE COMMAND SHIP'S HANGAR.
HAVE YOU NOTICED THAT THE SHIELDS ARE UP?
THOOM
OH! SORRY, MASTER.
SKREEEEEEE

ARTOO, STAY WITH THE SHIP.
I SENSE COUNT DOOKU...
I SENSE A *TRAP.*
NEXT MOVE?
SPRING THE TRAP.
GENERAL KENOBI. ANAKIN SKYWALKER. WE'VE BEEN WAITING FOR YOU.

WE ARE HERE TO RELIEVE YOU OF CHANCELLOR PALPATINE--
-- NOT JOIN HIM...
ANAKIN...
READY.
SPDOW!
VVVVSSSSSSSCHH
STOP THEM! DON'T LET THEM --
DON'T SHOOT! THAT LEVEL IS FILLED WITH --
FUEL...
THAT'S WHY THEY'VE STOPPED SHOOTING.
WELL THEN, WE'RE SAFE FOR THE TIME BEING.
YOUR IDEA OF "SAFE" IS NOT THE SAME AS MINE.

SUPER BATTLE DROIDS!
I FOUND OUR ESCAPE VENT.
IF THE FUEL HITS THOSE DISCHARGERS...
THAT WON'T HOLD --
THE BLAST WILL BREAK THE HULL. THIS SIDE'S PRESSURIZED.
"YOU STILL HAVE MUCH TO LEARN, ANAKIN."
BOOM!
ALL RIGHT, I STILL HAVE MUCH TO LEARN. LET'S GO!
HE'S CLOSE.
THE CHANCELLOR?
NO, COUNT DOOKU...

CHANCELLOR!
ARE YOU ALL RIGHT?
ANAKIN, DROIDS.
I WAS ABOUT TO SAY THAT.
THIS TIME WE DO IT TOGETHER.
YOUR SWORDS, PLEASE, MASTER JEDI. LET'S NOT MAKE A MESS OF THIS IN FRONT OF THE CHANCELLOR.
YOU WILL NOT ESCAPE THIS TIME, DOOKU!
MY POWERS HAVE DOUBLED SINCE WE LAST MET, COUNT.
GOOD! TWICE THE PRIDE, DOUBLE THE FALL. I HAVE LOOKED FORWARD TO THIS, SKYWALKER!

YOUR MOVES ARE CLUMSY, KENOBI--
GAH!
-- TOO PREDICTABLE.
NO!

I SENSE GREAT FEAR IN YOU, SKYWALKER. YOU HAVE POWER, YOU HAVE ANGER, BUT YOU DON'T USE THEM.
USE YOUR AGGRESSIVE FEELINGS, ANAKIN! CALL ON YOUR RAGE!
FOCUS IT!
SWIK!

GOOD, ANAKIN, GOOD! I KNEW YOU COULD DO IT! KILL HIM.
KILL HIM NOW!
PROTECT ME, CHANCELLOR...
DO IT!
I SHOULDN'T...

YOU DID WELL, ANAKIN. HE WAS TOO DANGEROUS TO BE KEPT ALIVE.
I SHOULDN'T HAVE DONE THAT. IT'S NOT THE JEDI WAY.
IT'S NOT THE FIRST TIME, ANAKIN. REMEMBER WHAT YOU TOLD ME ABOUT YOUR MOTHER AND THE SAND PEOPLE.
WE MUST LEAVE... THE SHIP IS FALLING OUT OF ORBIT.
THERE IS NO TIME. LEAVE HIM, OR WE'LL NEVER MAKE IT.
HIS FATE WILL BE THE SAME AS OURS.
HUHH... HAVE I MISSED SOMETHING? WHERE'S COUNT DOOKU?
DEAD.
PITY. ALIVE, HE COULD HAVE BEEN A HELP TO US.
THE SHIP'S BREAKING APART. COULD WE DISCUSS THIS LATER?

WE'LL HEAD TOWARD THE BRIDGE AND SEE IF WE CAN FIND AN ESCAPE POD.
UGH! RAY SHIELD!
THIS IS THE OLDEST TRAP IN THE BOOK...
I'M OPEN TO SUGGESTIONS HERE.
PERHAPS WITH COUNT DOOKU'S DEMISE, WE CAN NEGOTIATE OUR RELEASE.
I SAY... PATIENCE.
"PATIENCE"? THAT'S THE PLAN?
YEAH, THE DROIDS WILL RELEASE THE RAY SHIELD AND THEN WE'LL WIPE THEM OUT.
HAND OVER YOUR WEAPONS, JEDI!
I THINK CHANCELLOR PALPATINE'S SUGGESTION SOUNDS PRETTY GOOD TO ME.
WELL, WHAT'S PLAN B?

WELL, KENOBI, THAT WASN'T MUCH OF A RESCUE.
I THINK YOU'VE FORGOTTEN, GRIEVOUS -- I'M THE ONE IN CONTROL HERE.
OH, SO SURE OF YOURSELF, KENOBI --
-- BUT IT'S ALL OVER FOR YOU NOW --
I DON'T THINK SO!
ARGH!

CHUNK!
SIR, WE ARE FALLING OUT OF ORBIT. ALL AFT CONTROL CELLS ARE DEAD. THE SHIP IS BREAKING UP!
WE'VE RUN OUT OF TIME.
KRASH!
THE CONTROLS, ANAKIN!

"ANAKIN, THE HULL IS BURNING UP!"
"ALL THE ESCAPE PODS HAVE BEEN LAUNCHED."
"GRIEVOUS!"
YOU'RE THE HOTSHOT PILOT, ANAKIN -- DO YOU KNOW HOW TO FLY THIS TYPE OF CRUISER?
YOU MEAN, DO I KNOW HOW TO LAND WHAT'S LEFT OF THIS CRUISER!
WELL?
UNDER THE CIRCUMSTANCES, I'D SAY THE ABILITY TO PILOT THIS SHIP IS IRRELEVANT. STRAP YOURSELVES IN.

BLEET DO-BWEEP!
WE'VE GOT TO SLOW THIS WRECK DOWN, ARTOO. OPEN ALL HATCHES, EXTEND ALL FLAPS AND DRAG FINS.
STEADY...
KLIK!
ZZZZZZ!
"WE LOST SOMETHING."
EVERYTHING FROM THE HANGAR BACK JUST FELL OFF! ABOUT HALF THE SHIP, I'D SAY!
NOW WE'RE REALLY PICKING UP SPEED... I'M GOING TO SHIFT A FEW DEGREES AND SEE IF I CAN SLOW US DOWN.
CAREFUL... WE'RE HEATING UP!
FIRE SHIPS ARE ON THE LEFT AND RIGHT.
WE LOST OUR HEAT SHIELDS!

WE'RE COMING IN TOO HOT!

CHANCELLOR, ARE YOU ALL RIGHT?
I AM -- THANKS TO THESE TWO.

I KILLED COUNT DOOKU.
UNFORTUNATELY, GENERAL GRIEVOUS ESCAPED.
AND SO THE WAR WILL CONTINUE.
WITHOUT COUNT DOOKU THE SEPARATISTS ARE LEADERLESS. NOW IS THE TIME TO SUE FOR PEACE.
NONSENSE, MASTER WINDU! WITH GRIEVOUS STILL ALIVE, THEIR ABILITY TO WAGE WAR HAS NEVER BEEN STRONGER.
THEN WE WILL TRACK DOWN GRIEVOUS AND DESTROY HIM. THIS WAR MUST END!
WHAT IF MASTER YODA'S FEELINGS ARE CORRECT, AND COUNT DOOKU WAS MERELY THE APPRENTICE TO THE SITH LORD?
THAT'S A QUESTION ONLY TIME WILL REVEAL.
MY JEDI FRIENDS --
-- DON'T UNDERESTIMATE THE DEVIOUSNESS OF THE SEPARATISTS. I FEAR THIS WAR IS ONLY ONE MORE STEP IN A GREATER GAME.

ARE YOU COMING, MASTER?

I'M NOT **BRAVE ENOUGH** FOR POLITICS. I HAVE TO BRIEF THE COUNCIL.

THE SENATE CANNOT THANK YOU ENOUGH. THE END OF COUNT DOOKU WILL SURELY BRING AN END TO THIS WAR, AND AN END TO THE CHANCELLOR'S **DRACONIAN** SECURITY MEASURES.
I WISH THAT WERE SO, BUT THE FIGHTING IS GOING TO **CONTINUE** UNTIL GENERAL GRIEVOUS IS SPARE PARTS...

...THE CHANCELLOR IS **VERY** CLEAR ABOUT THAT.
EXCUSE ME.
THANK **GOODNESS,** YOU'RE BACK!
I'VE MISSED YOU SO.

THERE WERE WHISPERS THAT YOU'D BEEN KILLED. I'VE BEEN LIVING WITH ***UNBEARABLE*** DREAD.
I'M ALL RIGHT.

WAIT, NOT HERE...
NOT ***HERE?***
I'M ***TIRED*** OF THIS DECEPTION. I DON'T ***CARE*** IF THEY KNOW WE'RE MARRIED!

THE PLANET UTAPAU.
THE PLANET IS SECURE, SIR. THE POPULATION IS UNDER CONTROL.
GOOD. I MUST SPEAK TO THE SEPARATIST COUNCIL.
IT WON'T BE LONG BEFORE THE ARMIES OF THE REPUBLIC TRACK US HERE. MAKE YOUR WAY TO THE MUSTAFAR SYSTEM IN THE OUTER RIM. YOU WILL BE SAFE THERE.
SAFE?
CHAN-CELLOR PALPATINE MANAGED TO ESCAPE YOUR GRIP, GENERAL. I HAVE DOUBTS ABOUT YOUR ABILITY TO KEEP US SAFE.
BE THANK-FUL, VICEROY, YOU HAVE NOT FOUND YOURSELF IN MY GRIP. YOUR SHIP IS WAITING.
HAVE YOU MOVED THE SEPARATIST COUNCIL TO MUSTAFAR?
YES, MASTER.
THE JEDI WILL EXHAUST THEIR RESOURCES LOOKING FOR YOU. I DO NOT WISH THEM TO KNOW OF YOUR WHEREABOUTS UNTIL WE ARE READY.
THE END OF THE WAR IS NEAR, GENERAL, AND I PROMISE YOU, VICTORY IS ASSURED.
BUT THE LOSS OF COUNT DOOKU?
THE DEATH OF LORD TYRANUS WAS A NECESSARY LOSS, WHICH WILL ENSURE OUR VICTORY. I WILL SOON HAVE A NEW APPRENTICE ... ONE YOUNGER -- AND MORE POWERFUL.
CONTINUED!

HELP ME, ANAKIN!
UHH!
ANAKIN? WHAT'S BOTHERING YOU?
NOTHING. IT WAS A DREAM...
...LIKE THE ONES I USED TO HAVE ABOUT MY MOTHER JUST BEFORE SHE DIED.
IT WAS ABOUT YOU.
YOU DIE IN CHILDBIRTH...

AND THE BABY?
I DON'T KNOW.
IT WAS ONLY A DREAM.
I WON'T LET THIS ONE BECOME REAL.
THIS BABY WILL CHANGE OUR LIVES. I DOUBT THE QUEEN WILL CONTINUE TO ALLOW ME TO SERVE IN THE SENATE, AND IF THE COUNCIL DISCOVERS YOU ARE THE FATHER, YOU WILL BE EXPELLED FROM THE JEDI ORDER.
DO YOU THINK OBI-WAN MIGHT BE ABLE TO HELP US?
HAVE YOU TOLD HIM ANYTHING?
NO, BUT HE'S YOUR BEST FRIEND... HE MUST SUSPECT SOMETHING.
HE'S STILL ON THE COUNCIL. DON'T TELL HIM ANYTHING!
WE DON'T NEED HIS HELP. OUR BABY IS A BLESSING, NOT A PROBLEM.

MOVING TO TAKE CONTROL OF THE JEDI, THE CHANCELLOR IS.
I SENSE A PLOT TO DESTROY THE JEDI. THE DARK SIDE OF THE FORCE SURROUNDS THE CHANCELLOR.
AS IT SURROUNDS THE SEPARATISTS.
THERE IS A SHIFTING OF THE FORCE ... ALL OF US FEEL IT. IF THE CHANCELLOR IS BEING INFLUENCED BY THE DARK SIDE, THEN THIS WAR MAY BE A PLOT BY THE SITH TO TAKE OVER THE REPUBLIC.
SPECULATION! PROOF WE NEED, BEFORE TAKING THIS TO THE COUNCIL.
IF THE CHANCELLOR DOES NOT END THIS WAR WITH THE DESTRUCTION OF GENERAL GRIEVOUS, HE MUST BE REMOVED FROM OFFICE.
LATER...
I WAS HELD UP --
WHAT'S WRONG, THEN?
SALEUCAMI HAS FALLEN, AND MASTER VOS HAS MOVED HIS TROOPS TO BOZ PITY.
THE SENATE IS EXPECTED TO VOTE MORE EXECUTIVE POWERS TO THE CHANCELLOR TODAY.

IS THAT BAD? IT WILL MAKE IT EASIER FOR US TO END THIS WAR.
ANAKIN, BE CAREFUL OF YOUR FRIEND THE CHANCELLOR. HE HAS REQUESTED YOUR PRESENCE. HE WOULDN'T SAY WHY.
ALL OF THIS IS UNUSUAL, AND IT'S MAKING ME FEEL UNEASY.
RELATIONS BETWEEN THE COUNCIL AND THE CHANCELLOR ARE STRESSED.
I KNOW THE COUNCIL HAS GROWN WARY OF THE CHANCELLOR'S POWER. MINE ALSO, FOR THAT MATTER. AREN'T WE ALL WORKING TOGETHER TO SAVE THE REPUBLIC? WHY ALL THIS DISTRUST?
"THE FORCE GROWS DARK, ANAKIN, AND WE ARE ALL AFFECTED BY IT. BE WARY OF YOUR FEELINGS."
THIS AFTERNOON THE SENATE IS GOING TO CALL ON ME TO TAKE CONTROL OF THE JEDI COUNCIL.
THE JEDI WILL NO LONGER REPORT TO THE SENATE?
THEY WILL REPORT TO ME ... PERSONALLY. THE SENATE IS TOO UNFOCUSED TO CONDUCT A WAR. THIS WILL BRING A QUICK END TO THINGS.
WITH ALL DUE RESPECT, SIR, THE COUNCIL IS IN NO MOOD FOR MORE CONSTITUTIONAL AMENDMENTS.
IN THIS CASE I HAVE NO CHOICE ... THIS WAR MUST BE WON.

ANAKIN, I'VE KNOWN YOU SINCE YOU WERE A SMALL BOY.
I HAVE ADVISED YOU OVER THE YEARS WHEN I COULD. I AM VERY *PROUD* OF YOUR ACCOMPLISHMENTS.
IT'S UPSETTING TO ME THAT THE COUNCIL DOES NOT SEEM TO FULLY APPRECIATE YOUR TALENTS. DON'T YOU WONDER *WHY* YOU'VE BEEN KEPT OFF THE COUNCIL?
MY TIME *WILL* COME... WHEN I AM OLDER, AND, I SUPPOSE, WISER.
I THINK THEY SEE SOMETHING IN YOU THEY *FEAR.*
THEY SEE YOUR FUTURE --
-- AND THEY KNOW YOUR POWER WILL BE TOO STRONG FOR THEM TO CONTROL. THEY SEE YOU AS A *THREAT* TO *THEIR* POWER.
I NEED YOUR *HELP,* SON.
I CAN ASSURE YOU ARE JEDI ARE DEDICATED TO THE VALUES OF THE REPUBLIC.
I *FEAR* THE JEDI. THE COUNCIL KEEPS PUSHING FOR MORE CONTROL. THEY'RE SHROUDED IN SECRECY AND OBSESSED WITH MAINTAINING THEIR AUTONOMY.
NEVERTHELESS, THEIR *ACTIONS* WILL SPEAK LOUDER THAN THEIR WORDS. I'M *DEPENDING* ON YOU.
I'M APPOINTING YOU TO BE MY *PERSONAL REPRESENTATIVE* ON THE JEDI COUNCIL.
ME?! A *MASTER?* BUT THE COUNCIL ELECTS ITS OWN MEMBERS. THEY WILL *NEVER* ACCEPT THIS.

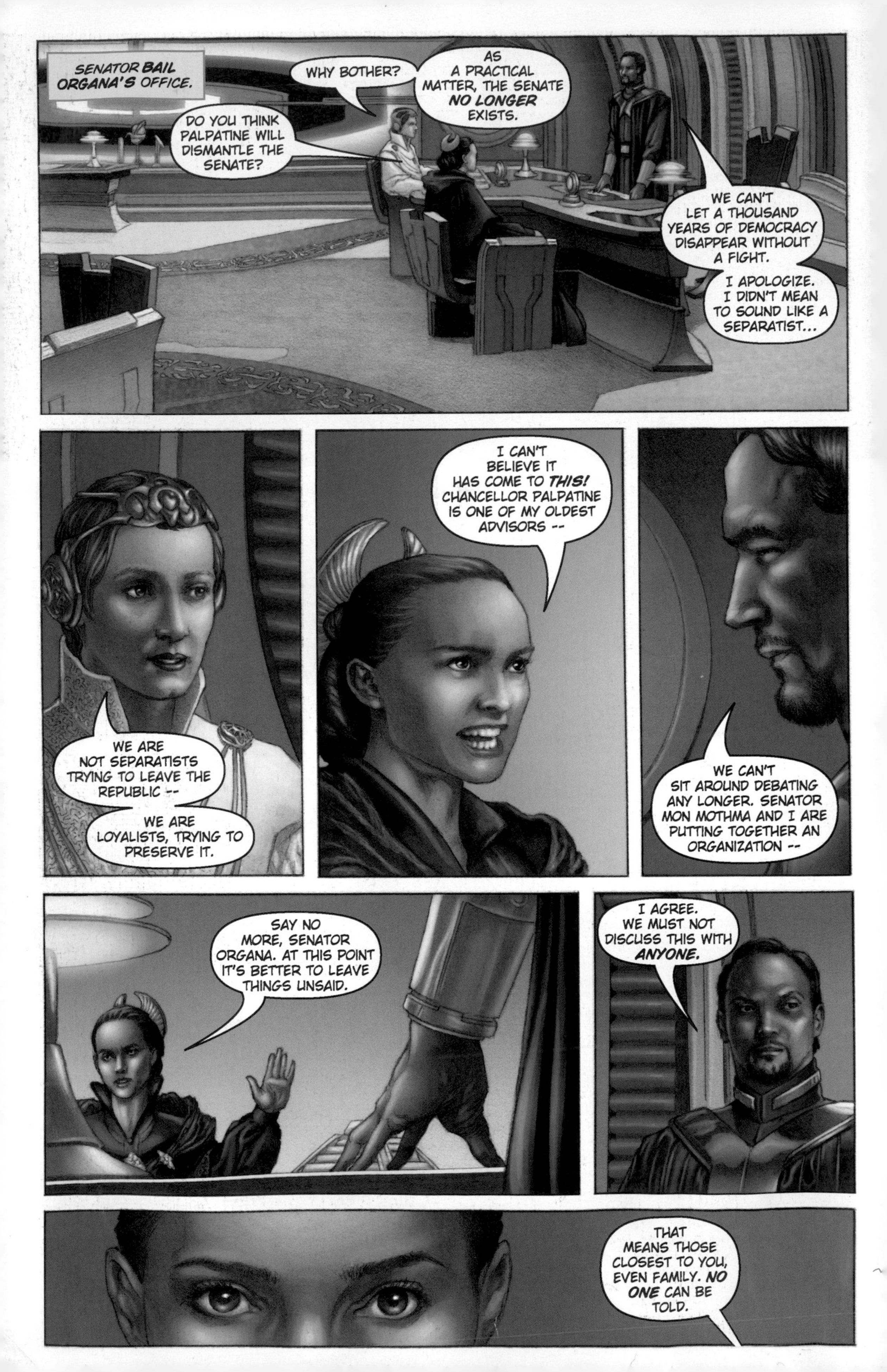
SENATOR BAIL ORGANA'S OFFICE.
DO YOU THINK PALPATINE WILL DISMANTLE THE SENATE?
WHY BOTHER?
AS A PRACTICAL MATTER, THE SENATE NO LONGER EXISTS.
WE CAN'T LET A THOUSAND YEARS OF DEMOCRACY DISAPPEAR WITHOUT A FIGHT.
I APOLOGIZE. I DIDN'T MEAN TO SOUND LIKE A SEPARATIST...
WE ARE NOT SEPARATISTS TRYING TO LEAVE THE REPUBLIC --
WE ARE LOYALISTS, TRYING TO PRESERVE IT.
I CAN'T BELIEVE IT HAS COME TO THIS! CHANCELLOR PALPATINE IS ONE OF MY OLDEST ADVISORS --
WE CAN'T SIT AROUND DEBATING ANY LONGER. SENATOR MON MOTHMA AND I ARE PUTTING TOGETHER AN ORGANIZATION --
SAY NO MORE, SENATOR ORGANA. AT THIS POINT IT'S BETTER TO LEAVE THINGS UNSAID.
I AGREE. WE MUST NOT DISCUSS THIS WITH ANYONE.
THAT MEANS THOSE CLOSEST TO YOU, EVEN FAMILY. NO ONE CAN BE TOLD.

ANAKIN SKYWALKER, WE HAVE APPROVED YOUR APPOINTMENT TO THE COUNCIL AS THE CHANCELLOR'S PERSONAL REPRESENTATIVE.
ALLOW THIS APPOINTMENT LIGHTLY, THE COUNCIL DOES NOT. DISTURBING IS THIS MOVE BY CHANCELLOR PALPATINE.
YOU ARE ON THE COUNCIL, BUT WE DO NOT GRANT YOU THE RANK OF MASTER.
WHAT?! HOW CAN YOU DO THIS? I'M MORE POWERFUL THAN ANY OF YOU! HOW CAN I BE ON THE COUNCIL AND NOT BE A MASTER...?
ANAKIN!
I ... FORGIVE ME, MASTER.
TAKE YOUR SEAT, YOUNG SKYWALKER.
WE HAVE SURVEYED ALL SYSTEMS IN THE REPUBLIC AND HAVE FOUND NO SIGN OF GENERAL GRIEVOUS.
HIDING IN THE OUTER RIM, HE IS. CONTACT OUR SPIES, MASTER KENOBI MUST. THEN WAIT.
WHAT OF THE DROID LANDING ON KASHYYYK?
I KNOW THAT SYSTEM WELL. IT WOULD TAKE US LITTLE TIME TO DRIVE THE DROIDS OFF THAT PLANET.
SKYWALKER, YOUR ASSIGNMENT IS HERE WITH THE CHANCELLOR. KENOBI MUST FIND GRIEVOUS.
GOOD RELATIONS WITH THE WOOKIEES, I HAVE. GO, I WILL.
IT IS SETTLED THEN.

WHAT KIND OF NONSENSE IS THIS, PUT ME ON THE COUNCIL AND NOT MAKE ME A MASTER!? IT'S INSULTING!
YOU'VE BEEN GIVEN A GREAT HONOR. TO BE ON THE COUNCIL AT YOUR AGE HAS NEVER HAPPENED BEFORE. ANAKIN, THE FACT IS YOU'RE TOO CLOSE TO THE CHANCELLOR, AND THE COUNCIL DOESN'T LIKE HIM INTERFERING IN JEDI AFFAIRS.
I DIDN'T ASK TO BE PUT ON THE COUNCIL...
BUT IT'S WHAT YOU WANTED! YOUR FRIENDSHIP WITH CHANCELLOR PALPATINE SEEMS TO HAVE PAID OFF. YOU FIND YOURSELF IN A DELICATE SITUATION...
YOU MEAN DIVIDED LOYALTIES.
I WARNED YOU THERE WAS TENSION BETWEEN THE COUNCIL AND THE CHANCELLOR. WHY DIDN'T YOU LISTEN? YOU WALKED RIGHT INTO IT.
THE COUNCIL IS UPSET BECAUSE I'M THE YOUNGEST TO EVER SERVE.
NO, IT IS NOT.
ANAKIN, I WORRY WHEN YOU SPEAK OF JEALOUSY AND PRIDE. THOSE ARE NOT JEDI THOUGHTS. THEY'RE DANGEROUS, DARK THOUGHTS.
MASTER, YOU OF ALL PEOPLE SHOULD HAVE CONFIDENCE IN MY ABILITIES. I KNOW WHERE MY LOYALTIES LIE. I SENSE THERE'S MORE TO THIS TALK THAN YOU'RE SAYING.
WE ARE AT WAR, ANAKIN! THE JEDI COUNCIL IS SWORN TO UPHOLD THE PRINCIPLES OF THE REPUBLIC, EVEN IF THE CHANCELLOR DOES NOT.
YOU MUST REPORT PALPATINE'S ACTIVITIES TO THE COUNCIL.
THEY WANT ME TO SPY ON THE CHANCELLOR? THAT'S TREASON!

...HE'S WATCHED OUT FOR ME EVER SINCE I ARRIVED HERE.
THAT IS WHY YOU MUST HELP US.
WE OWE OUR ALLEGIANCE TO THE SENATE, NOT TO ITS LEADER, WHO HAS MANAGED TO STAY IN OFFICE LONG AFTER HIS TERM HAS EXPIRED.
USE YOUR FEELINGS, ANAKIN! SOMETHING IS OUT OF PLACE HERE.
YOU'RE ASKING ME TO DO SOMETHING AGAINST THE JEDI CODE. AGAINST THE REPUBLIC. AGAINST A MENTOR... AND A FRIEND.
"THAT'S WHAT'S OUT OF PLACE HERE."
ANAKIN DID NOT TAKE TO HIS ASSIGNMENT WITH MUCH ENTHUSIASM.
TOO MUCH UNDER THE SWAY OF THE CHANCELLOR, HE IS. MUCH ANGER THERE IS IN HIM. TOO MUCH PRIDE IN HIS POWERS.
THIS IS A DANGEROUS MOVE, PUTTING THEM TOGETHER. I DON'T TRUST ANAKIN.
ANAKIN WILL NOT LET ME DOWN. HE NEVER HAS.
RIGHT, I HOPE YOU ARE.
AND NOW, DESTROY THE DROID ARMIES ON KASHYYYK, I WILL. MAY THE FORCE BE WITH YOU.

I HEARD ABOUT YOUR APPOINTMENT, ANAKIN. I'M SO *PROUD* OF YOU.
I MAY BE ON THE COUNCIL, BUT THEY REFUSED TO ACCEPT ME AS A JEDI MASTER. THEY *FEAR* MY POWER, THAT'S THE PROBLEM.
SOMETIMES I WONDER WHAT'S HAPPENING TO THE JEDI ORDER. I THINK THIS WAR IS DESTROYING THE PRINCIPLES OF THE REPUBLIC.
HAVE YOU EVER CONSIDERED THAT WE MAY BE ON THE *WRONG* SIDE?
WHAT IF THE DEMOCRACY WE THOUGHT WE WERE SERVING NO LONGER EXISTS, AND THE REPUBLIC HAS BECOME THE VERY EVIL WE HAVE BEEN FIGHTING TO DESTROY?
I *DON'T* BELIEVE THAT, PADMÉ. YOU'RE SOUNDING LIKE A SEPARATIST!
THIS WAR REPRESENTS A FAILURE TO LISTEN!
YOU'RE CLOSER TO THE CHANCELLOR THAN ANYONE. *PLEASE* ASK HIM TO STOP THE FIGHTING AND LET DIPLOMACY RESUME.

DON'T ASK ME TO DO THAT, PADMÉ. I'M *NOT* YOUR ERRAND BOY. I'M NOT *ANYONE'S* ERRAND BOY!
DON'T SHUT ME OUT, LET ME *HELP* YOU.
I'M TRYING TO HELP *YOU.*

HOLD ME, LIKE YOU DID BY THE LAKE ON NABOO SO LONG AGO. WHEN THERE WAS NO POLITICS, NO PLOTTING...
...NO WAR.

THE GALAXIES OPERA HOUSE.
YOU WANTED TO SEE ME, CHANCELLOR?
YES, ANAKIN. YOU KNOW I'M NOT ABLE TO RELY ON THE JEDI COUNCIL. YOU MUST SENSE WHAT I'VE COME TO SUSPECT...
THE JEDI COUNCIL WANTS CONTROL OF THE REPUBLIC. THEY'RE PLANNING TO BETRAY ME.
YOU KNOW, DON'T YOU?
I KNOW THEY DON'T TRUST YOU.
THEY ASKED YOU TO SPY ON ME, DIDN'T THEY?
"ALL THOSE WHO GAIN POWER ARE AFRAID TO LOSE IT." EVEN THE JEDI.
THE JEDI USE THEIR POWER FOR GOOD.
GOOD IS A POINT OF VIEW, ANAKIN. THE JEDI POINT OF VIEW IS NOT THE ONLY VALID ONE. THE DARK LORDS OF THE SITH BELIEVE IN SECURITY AND JUSTICE ALSO, YET THEY ARE CONSIDERED BY THE JEDI TO BE --
EVIL.

YET THE SITH AND THE JEDI ARE SIMILAR IN ALMOST EVERY WAY -- *INCLUDING* THEIR QUEST FOR GREATER POWER. THE *DIFFERENCE* BETWEEN THE TWO IS THAT THE SITH ARE *NOT AFRAID* OF THE DARK SIDE OF THE FORCE.
THAT IS WHY *THEY* ARE MORE POWERFUL.
THE SITH RELY ON THEIR PASSION FOR THEIR STRENGTH. THEY THINK *INWARD,* ONLY ABOUT THEMSELVES. THE JEDI ARE *SELFLESS* ... THEY ONLY CARE ABOUT *OTHERS.*
THE FEAR OF *LOSING* POWER IS A WEAKNESS OF *BOTH* THE JEDI AND THE SITH.
HAVE YOU EVER HEARD THE TRAGEDY OF *DARTH PLAGUEIS?*
HE WAS A DARK LORD OF THE SITH, SO POWERFUL AND WISE HE COULD USE THE FORCE TO *INFLUENCE* THE MIDI-CHLORIANS TO *CREATE LIFE.*
HE HAD SUCH KNOWLEDGE OF THE DARK SIDE THAT HE COULD EVEN KEEP THE ONES HE CARED ABOUT FROM DYING.
HE COULD ACTUALLY KEEP SOMEONE SAFE FROM *DEATH?*
HE TAUGHT HIS APPRENTICE EVERYTHING HE KNEW, AND THEN HIS APPRENTICE *KILLED HIM* IN HIS SLEEP. PLAGUEIS NEVER SAW IT COMING.
HE COULD SAVE *OTHERS* FROM DEATH, BUT NOT *HIMSELF.*
IS IT POSSIBLE TO *LEARN* THIS POWER?
NOT FROM A JEDI.

IT'S ANAKIN. HE'S BEEN PUT IN A DIFFICULT POSITION AS THE CHANCELLOR'S REPRESENTATIVE, BUT I THINK IT'S MORE THAN THAT. I WAS HOPING HE MIGHT HAVE TALKED TO YOU.
WHY WOULD HE TALK TO ME ABOUT HIS WORK?
I KNOW HOW HE FEELS ABOUT YOU, PADMÉ.
I DON'T KNOW WHAT YOU'RE TALKING ABOUT.
I CAN SEE YOU TWO ARE IN LOVE. I'M WORRIED ABOUT HIM. HE'S CHANGED CONSIDERABLY SINCE WE RETURNED...
BLEET
YES, MASTER WINDU?
OBI-WAN, GENERAL GRIEVOUS HAS BEEN LOCATED ON UTAPAU! PREPARE TWO CLONE BRIGADES.
I'M ON MY WAY!
I'M NOT TELLING THE COUNCIL ABOUT ANY OF THIS.
THANK YOU, OBI-WAN.
PLEASE DO WHAT YOU CAN TO HELP HIM.

"YOU'RE GOING TO NEED ME ON THIS ONE, MASTER."
"IT MAY BE NOTHING MORE THAN A WILD BANTHA CHASE, ANAKIN."
MASTER, I'VE DISAPPOINTED YOU. I HAVE BEEN ARROGANT. I APOLOGIZE.
I'M JUST SO FRUSTRATED WITH THE COUNCIL. YOUR FRIENDSHIP MEANS EVERYTHING TO ME.
YOU ARE WISE AND STRONG. I AM VERY PROUD OF YOU.
DON'T WORRY, I HAVE ENOUGH CLONES WITH ME TO TAKE THREE SYSTEMS THE SIZE OF UTAPAU. I THINK I'LL BE ABLE TO HANDLE THE SITUATION, EVEN WITHOUT YOUR HELP.
WELL, THERE'S ALWAYS A FIRST TIME.
GOOD-BYE, OLD FRIEND. MAY THE FORCE BE WITH YOU.
MAY THE FORCE BE WITH YOU.

A SHORT TIME LATER...
I SENSE SOMEONE FAMILIAR...
OBI-WAN'S BEEN HERE, HASN'T HE?
HE CAME BY THIS MORNING. HE'S WORRIED ABOUT YOU.
YOU TOLD HIM ABOUT US, DIDN'T YOU?
HE SAYS YOU'RE UNDER A LOT OF STRESS. YOU HAVE BEEN MOODY LATELY.
I'M NOT MOODY. I FEEL ... LOST.
OBI-WAN AND THE COUNCIL DON'T TRUST ME.
THEY TRUST YOU WITH THEIR LIVES. OBI-WAN LOVES YOU AS A SON.
I'M NOT THE JEDI I SHOULD BE. I AM ONE OF THE MOST POWERFUL, BUT I'M NOT SATISFIED. I WANT MORE, BUT I KNOW I SHOULDN'T.
I HAVE FOUND A WAY TO SAVE YOU. I AM BECOMING SO POWERFUL WITH MY NEW KNOWLEDGE OF THE FORCE, I WILL BE ABLE TO KEEP YOU FROM DYING.
IS THAT WHAT'S BOTHERING YOU? YOU DON'T NEED MORE POWER, ANAKIN. I BELIEVE YOU CAN PROTECT ME AGAINST ANYTHING...
JUST AS YOU ARE.

UTAPAU.
GREETINGS, YOUNG JEDI. WHAT BRINGS YOU TO OUR REMOTE SANCTUARY?
I WOULD LIKE SOME FUEL -- AND TO USE YOUR CITY AS A BASE TO SEARCH NEARBY SYSTEMS...
...FOR A DROID ARMY, LED BY GENERAL GRIEVOUS.
HE IS HERE! WE ARE BEING HELD HOSTAGE. THEY ARE WATCHING US. THE TENTH LEVEL. THOUSANDS OF BATTLE DROIDS...
I UNDERSTAND. HAVE YOUR PEOPLE SEEK SHELTER. IF YOU HAVE WARRIORS, NOW IS THE TIME.
GENERAL KENOBI REPORTS THAT HE HAS LOCATED GENERAL GRIEVOUS ON UTAPAU. WE'RE PREPARING TO ATTACK.
THANK YOU, COMMANDER.
ANAKIN, I HAVE A VERY IMPORTANT ASSIGNMENT FOR YOU.
MASTER?

"GO TO THE SUPREME CHANCELLOR. TELL HIM THAT GENERAL GRIEVOUS HAS BEEN FOUND. WATCH HIS REACTIONS CLOSELY. THROUGH THEM WE MAY DISCOVER THE CHANCELLOR'S TRUE INTENTIONS. THEN REPORT BACK TO ME."
THE TENTH LEVEL...
I NEED TRANSPORTATION. GET IT FOR ME.
YOU NEED TRANSPORTATION.
I WILL GET IT FOR YOU.
BOGA, SHE ANSWERS TO BOGA.
GOOD GIRL, BOGA.

HUH...?
GENERAL KENOBI. YOU ARE A BOLD ONE.
BUT SURELY YOU REALIZE YOU'RE DOOMED.
NOT THIS TIME!

ATTACK, KENOBI. I HAVE BEEN TRAINED IN YOUR JEDI ARTS BY **COUNT DOOKU** HIMSELF.

I HAVE **THOUSANDS** OF TROOPS. YOU WILL **NOT** DEFEAT THEM.
I MAY NOT DEFEAT YOUR DROIDS, BUT MY **TROOPS** CERTAINLY **WILL.**

THAK!
YOUR TROOPS WILL NEVER PENETRATE MY DEFENSES.
DON'T COUNT ON IT.
WOK!

NNGH!
OOF!
BOOW!
BOOW!
BOOW!

SO, MASTER KENOBI HAS LOCATED GENERAL GRIEVOUS. INTERESTING.
AND THE COUNCIL ASKED YOU TO REPORT ON MY REACTION TO THIS NEWS, DIDN'T THEY?
CHANCELLOR, THEY JUST WANT THIS WAR TO END -- AS EVERYONE DOES...
"IS THAT WHAT THEY TOLD YOU? AND DID YOU BELIEVE THEM?
"ANAKIN, YOU MUST BREAK THROUGH THE FOG OF LIES THE JEDI HAVE CREATED AROUND YOU. LET ME HELP YOU TO LEARN THE TRUE WAYS OF THE FORCE."
"CHANCELLOR -- H-HOW DO YOU KNOW THE WAYS OF THE FORCE?"
MY MENTOR TAUGHT ME EVERYTHING ABOUT THE FORCE...
...EVEN THE NATURE OF THE DARK SIDE.
TO BE CONTINUED!

YOU'RE A SITH LORD!
I AM. BUT I AM NOT YOUR ENEMY, ANAKIN.
I NEED YOUR HELP TO RESTORE PEACE TO THE GALAXY.
HELP YOU?! I SHOULD KILL YOU!
I KNOW YOU WOULD LIKE TO. YOU'VE BEEN SEARCHING FOR A LIFE GREATER THAN THAT OF AN ORDINARY JEDI.
I WON'T BE A PAWN IN YOUR POLITICAL GAME. THE JEDI ARE MY FAMILY.
BUT YOU'RE NOT SURE OF THEIR INTENTIONS, ARE YOU? WHAT IF I AM RIGHT, AND THEY ARE PLOTTING TO TAKE OVER THE REPUBLIC?
THEY FEAR YOU. IN TIME THEY WILL DESTROY YOU. LET ME TRAIN YOU -- SHOW YOU THE TRUE NATURE OF THE FORCE.
LEARN TO CONTROL THE DARK SIDE AND YOU WILL BE ABLE TO SAVE YOUR WIFE FROM CERTAIN DEATH.

I WON'T BECOME A SITH!
I CAN FEEL YOUR ANGER. IT GIVES YOU FOCUS, MAKES YOU STRONGER.
WILL YOU KILL ME IF IT MEANS PLUNGING THE GALAXY INTO ETERNAL CHAOS AND STRIFE?
I AM GOING TO TURN YOU OVER TO THE JEDI COUNCIL ... I WILL DISCOVER THE TRUTH OF ALL THIS.
YOU HAVE GREAT WISDOM, ANAKIN. I WANT YOU TO MEDIATE ON MY PROPOSAL TO KNOW THE POWER OF THE DARK SIDE.
THE POWER TO SAVE PADMÉ.
UTAPAU.
SEND A MESSAGE TO CORUSCANT. GENERAL GRIEVOUS IS DEAD.
YES, SIR!

THE JEDI TEMPLE HANGAR...
NOW THAT GENERAL GRIEVOUS HAS BEEN KILLED, IT'S TIME PALPATINE ENDED THIS WAR.
PREPARE YOURSELVES, THE SITH LORD COULD BE ANYWHERE. I HAVE A FEELING PALPATINE WILL NOT SURRENDER HIS POWER EASILY, OR WITHOUT A FIGHT.
ANAKIN --?! WHAT'S WRONG?
MASTERS... IT'S CHANCELLOR PALPATINE...
SKYWALKER, WHAT HAVE YOU LEARNED?
PALPATINE ... PALPATINE IS THE SITH LORD!
HE TOLD ME. HE KNOWS THE WAYS OF THE DARK SIDE...
THEN OUR WORST FEARS ARE TRUE.
LET ME GO WITH YOU...
HE'S TOO POWERFUL. YOU'LL NEED ME!
NO, ANAKIN! I SENSE MUCH CONFLICT IN YOU. STAY HERE AND MEDITATE ON THIS.
STAY HERE. THAT'S AN ORDER, ANAKIN.

CHANCELLOR, THIS WAR IS OVER.
THE JEDI WILL NOT CONTINUE TO BE YOUR PERSONAL EXECUTIONERS.
THE WAR ISN'T OVER. THE SEPARATIST LEADERSHIP MUST BE DESTROYED. AN EXAMPLE MUST BE MADE.
THE JEDI WILL DO WHAT THEY'RE TOLD!
YOU'RE UNDER ARREST, CHANCELLOR.
YOU ARE TRAITORS TO THE REPUBLIC --
-- I WILL NOT TOLERATE YOUR TREASON!

I WON'T LET YOU DIE, PADMÉ.
I WON'T!

SUPREME CHANCELLOR ... MASTER WINDU...
YOU ARE WELL-VERSED IN THE WAYS OF THE JEDI, BUT YOU ARE NO JEDI!
ANAKIN, HELP ME!
HE'S TOO STRONG!
ANAKIN, HE'S A TRAITOR! HE'LL BETRAY YOU JUST AS HE BETRAYED ME.
YOU'RE NOT ONE OF THEM, ANAKIN!
UNLIMITED POWER, ANAKIN ... HELP ME!
HELP ME...

...
ANAKIN ... WE MUST FINISH HIM. HERE. NOW! BEFORE HE KILLS US ALL!
NO! HE MUST BE KEPT ALIVE!
HE'S TOO DANGEROUS!
GAHH!
ANAKIN ... ?

WHAT HAVE I DONE?
YOU'RE FOLLOWING YOUR DESTINY.
I NEED YOU TO HELP ME BRING ORDER TO THE GALAXY.
THINK ABOUT PADMÉ. I CAN HELP YOU SAVE HER. BECOME MY APPRENTICE.
I WANT THE POWER TO STOP DEATH.
YOU WERE RIGHT. THE JEDI BETRAYED BOTH OF US.
I PLEDGE MYSELF TO THE WAYS OF THE SITH.
ANAKIN SKYWALKER, YOU ARE ONE WITH THE ORDER OF THE SITH LORDS.
HENCEFORTH, YOU SHALL BE KNOWN AS ... DARTH VADER.
GO TO THE JEDI TEMPLE. DO WHAT MUST BE DONE, LORD VADER. SHOW NO MERCY.
THEN GO TO THE MUSTAFAR SYSTEM. WIPE OUT THE SEPARATIST LEADERS, AND --

Beedeep
"-- ONCE MORE THE SITH WILL RULE THE GALAXY ... AND WE SHALL HAVE PEACE."
EXECUTE ORDER SIXTY-SIX.
IT WILL BE DONE, MY LORD.
MYGEETO.
COMMANDER BACARRA, EXECUTE ORDER SIXTY-SIX.
GENERAL...
BKOW!

FELUCIA.
IT GOT QUIET SUDDENLY...
BLY, DO YOU THINK IT'S DROIDS?
NO.

KASHYYYK.
UTAPAU.
DOW!
DOW!
DOW!

KASHYYYK.

I SENSE A GREAT DISTURBANCE IN THE FORCE.

STAY ALERT...

CORUSCANT.
WHAT'S GOING ON?!
THERE'S BEEN A REBELLION, SIR.

WHAT?! THAT'S *IMPOSSIBLE!*
THE SITUATION IS UNDER CONTROL.
BUT *NO ONE* IS ALLOWED ENTRY.
SKATZ!
DOW! DOW!

BDOW! BDOW!
DOW!

DON'T BOTHER --
-- HE'S NOT A JEDI.

MY LADY, THERE'S A JEDI FIGHTER DOCKING ON THE VERANDA.
I CAME TO MAKE SURE YOU AND THE BABY ARE SAFE.
THE SITUATION IS NOT GOOD. THE JEDI COUNCIL HAS TRIED TO OVERTHROW THE REPUBLIC.
I CAN'T BELIEVE THAT!
I SAW MASTER WINDU ATTEMPT TO ASSASSINATE THE CHANCELLOR MYSELF.
W-WHAT ARE YOU GOING TO DO?
I WILL NOT BETRAY THE REPUBLIC. MY LOYALTIES LIE WITH THE CHANCELLOR AND THE SENATE ... AND WITH YOU.
WHAT ABOUT OBI-WAN?
I DON'T KNOW ... MANY OF THE JEDI HAVE BEEN KILLED.
HOW COULD THIS HAVE HAPPENED?
THE REPUBLIC IS UNSTABLE, PADME. THE JEDI AREN'T THE ONLY ONES TRYING TO TAKE ADVANTAGE OF THE SITUATION.
THERE ARE ALSO TRAITORS IN THE SENATE.

WHAT ARE YOU SAYING?
YOU NEED TO DISTANCE YOURSELF FROM YOUR FRIENDS IN THE SENATE. THE CHANCELLOR SAID THEY WILL BE DEALT WITH WHEN THIS CONFLICT IS OVER.
I'VE OPPOSED THIS WAR. WHAT WILL YOU DO IF I BECOME A SUSPECT?
THAT WON'T HAPPEN. I WON'T LET IT.
I WANT TO LEAVE. GO SOMEPLACE FAR FROM HERE.
I WANT TO BRING UP OUR CHILD SOMEPLACE SAFE.
I WANT THAT TOO. BUT THAT PLACE IS HERE. THINGS ARE DIFFERENT NOW. THERE IS A NEW ORDER. SOON I WILL BE ABLE TO PROTECT YOU FROM ANY-THING.
OH, ANAKIN, I'M AFRAID.
HAVE FAITH, MY LOVE. EVERYTHING WILL BE SET RIGHT.
THE SEPARATISTS HAVE GATHERED IN THE MUSTAFAR SYSTEM. I'M GOING THERE TO END THIS WAR. WAIT UNTIL I RETURN...

"...THINGS WILL BE DIFFERENT, I PROMISE."
WERE YOU ABLE TO GET HOLD OF A JEDI HOMING BEACON?
YES, SIR. WE'VE ENCOUNTERED NO OPPOSITION. THE CLONES ARE STILL CONFUSED. IT APPEARS NO ONE IS IN COMMAND.
THAT WILL CHANGE SOON. HOPEFULLY WE CAN INTERCEPT A FEW JEDI BEFORE THEY WALK INTO THIS CATASTROPHE...
CHEWBACCA AND TARFFUL, GOOD FRIENDS ARE. FOR YOUR HELP, MUCH GRATITUDE AND RESPECT, I HAVE.

EMERGENCY CODE NINE THIRTEEN ... ARE THERE ANY JEDI OUT THERE?
ANYWHERE?
BZZT ›FSSSSSHH‹ KRACKLE!
I'VE LOCKED ON! REPEAT.
MASTER KENOBI?
SENATOR ORGANA! MY CLONE TROOPS TURNED ON ME ... I NEED HELP.
IT APPEARS THIS AMBUSH HAS HAPPENED EVERYWHERE. LOCK ON TO MY COORDINATES.

LATER.

YOU MADE IT.
MASTER KENOBI, DARK TIMES ARE THESE. GOOD TO SEE YOU, IT IS.
YOU WERE ATTACKED BY YOUR TROOPS ALSO?
WITH THE HELP OF THE WOOKIEES, BARELY ESCAPE, I DID.
HOW MANY MORE JEDI MANAGED TO SURVIVE?
WE'VE HEARD FROM NONE.
I SAW THOUSANDS OF TROOPS ATTACK THE JEDI TEMPLE.
FROM THE TEMPLE, RECEIVED THE CODED RETREAT SIGNAL, WE HAVE.
IT REQUESTS ALL JEDI RETURN TO CORUSCANT. THE WAR IS OVER...
WE HAVE TO GO BACK!
IF THERE ARE OTHER STRAGGLERS, THEY WILL FALL INTO THE TRAP AND BE KILLED.

SUGGEST DISMANTLING THE CODED SIGNAL, DO YOU?
YES, THERE'S *TOO MUCH* AT STAKE HERE, MASTER. WE NEED A CLEARER PICTURE OF WHAT HAS HAPPENED.
I AGREE. IN A DARK PLACE WE FIND OURSELVES. A LITTLE KNOWLEDGE MIGHT LIGHT OUR WAY.
MUSTAFAR.
ARTOO, STAY WITH THE SHIP.
BWOOP...
THE PLAN HAS GONE AS YOU HAD PROMISED, MY LORD.
YOU HAVE DONE WELL, VICEROY. HAVE YOU SHUT DOWN YOUR DROID ARMIES?

WE HAVE, MY LORD.
EXCELLENT! HAS MY NEW APPRENTICE, DARTH VADER, ARRIVED?
HE LANDED A FEW MOMENTS AGO.
GOOD. HE WILL TAKE CARE OF YOU.

THE WAR IS OVER. LORD SIDIOUS PROMISED US PEACE --
TO BE CONCLUDED!

THE JEDI'S ATTEMPT ON MY LIFE HAS LEFT ME SCARRED AND DEFORMED, BUT I ASSURE YOU, MY RESOLVE HAS NEVER BEEN STRONGER.
THE REMAINING JEDI WILL BE HUNTED DOWN AND DEFEATED. ANY COLLABORATORS WILL SUFFER THE SAME FATE.
THE WAR IS OVER. THE SEPARATISTS HAVE BEEN ELIMINATED AND THE JEDI REBELLION HAS BEEN FOILED.
WE STAND ON THE THRESHOLD OF A NEW BEGINNING.
IN ORDER TO ENSURE OUR SECURITY AND STABILITY, THE REPUBLIC WILL BE REORGANIZED INTO THE FIRST GALACTIC EMPIRE.
AN EMPIRE THAT WILL CONTINUE TO BE RULED BY THIS AUGUST BODY --
-- AND A SOVEREIGN RULER CHOSEN FOR LIFE!
HEAR! HEAR!
YEAH!
SO THIS IS HOW LIBERTY DIES, WITH THUNDEROUS APPLAUSE...
WE CANNOT LET THIS HAPPEN!
WE CAN DO NOTHING NOW. BUT THERE WILL BE A TIME...

"THERE ARE CLONE TROOPERS ON EVERY LEVEL, MANY DRESSED AS JEDI."
"DISMANTLE THE CODED SIGNAL QUICKLY, WE MUST."
NOT EVEN THE YOUNGLINGS SURVIVED.
I'VE RECALIBRATED THE CODE TO WARN ANY SURVIVING JEDI AWAY.
GOOD. TO DISCOVER THE RECALIBRATION, A LONG TIME IT WILL TAKE. TO CHANGE IT BACK, LONGER STILL.
THERE IS SOMETHING I MUST KNOW...
OBI-WAN, THE TRUTH YOU ALREADY KNOW...

IT CAN'T BE!
IT CAN'T BE...
YOU HAVE DONE WELL, MY NEW APPRENTICE. YOUR SKILLS ARE UNMATCHED BY ANY SITH BEFORE YOU. NOW GO, LORD VADER, AND BRING PEACE TO THE EMPIRE.
HOW COULD IT HAVE COME TO THIS?
DESTROY THE SITH, WE MUST.
SEND ME TO KILL THE EMPEROR. I WILL NOT KILL ANAKIN.
POWERFUL ENOUGH TO DESTROY THE EMPEROR, YOU ARE NOT.
ANAKIN IS LIKE MY BROTHER... I CANNOT DO THIS.
TWISTED BY THE DARK SIDE, YOUNG SKYWALKER HAS BECOME. THE BOY YOU TRAINED, GONE HE IS... CONSUMED BY DARTH VADER.
VISIT THE NEW EMPEROR, I MUST.

LATER...
OBI-WAN! THANK GOODNESS YOU'RE ALIVE!
THE REPUBLIC HAS FALLEN... THE JEDI ORDER IS NO MORE...
I BELIEVE WE HAVE BEEN PART OF A PLOT HUNDREDS OF YEARS IN THE MAKING.
I KNOW.
THE SENATE IS STILL INTACT. THERE IS SOME HOPE...
NO, PADMÉ... IT'S OVER.
THE SITH NOW RULE THE GALAXY AS THEY DID BEFORE THE REPUBLIC.
THE SITH?!
I'M LOOKING FOR ANAKIN... DO YOU KNOW WHERE HE IS?
PADMÉ, I NEED YOUR HELP. HE'S IN GRAVE DANGER.
ANAKIN HAS TURNED TO THE DARK SIDE.
HOW COULD YOU SAY THAT?!
I'VE SEEN A SECURITY HOLOGRAM OF HIM KILLING JEDI YOUNGLINGS.
NOT ANAKIN! HE COULDN'T!
HE HAS BEEN DECEIVED, PADMÉ, AS WE ALL HAVE BEEN.
IT APPEARS THE CHANCELLOR -- THE EMPEROR -- IS BEHIND EVERYTHING, INCLUDING THE WAR.

PALPATINE IS THE SITH LORD WE'VE BEEN LOOKING FOR.
AFTER THE DEATH OF COUNT DOOKU, ANAKIN BECAME HIS NEW APPRENTICE. I MUST FIND HIM.
YOU'RE GOING TO KILL HIM, AREN'T YOU?
HE HAS BECOME A VERY GREAT THREAT.
ANAKIN'S THE FATHER, ISN'T HE?
I'M SO SORRY.
AND A SHORT WHILE LATER...

SENATE ARENA, CHANCELLOR'S OFFICE.
IT IS FINISHED, THEN. BY KILLING THE SEPARTIST LEADERS, YOU HAVE RESTORED PEACE AND JUSTICE TO THE GALAXY, LORD VADER.
THANK YOU, MY MASTER.
A NEW APPRENTICE YOU HAVE, CHANCELLOR. OR SHOULD I CALL YOU EMPEROR.
MASTER YODA, YOU SURVIVED.
SURPRISED?
YOUR ARROGANCE BLINDS YOU, YODA. NOW YOU WILL EXPERIENCE THE FULL POWER OF THE DARK SIDE.
I HAVE WAITED A LONG TIME FOR THIS MOMENT, MY LITTLE GREEN FRIEND.
THE JEDI ARE NO MORE. AT LAST THE SITH WILL RULE THE GALAXY!
NOT IF ANYTHING I HAVE TO SAY ABOUT IT, LORD SIDIOUS!
AT AN END YOUR RULE IS...

MUSTAFAR.
PADMÉ! I SAW YOUR SHIP...

OH, ANAKIN!
IT'S ALL RIGHT, YOU'RE SAFE NOW. WHAT ARE YOU DOING OUT HERE?
I WAS SO WORRIED ABOUT YOU. OBI-WAN TOLD ME TERRIBLE THINGS. HE SAID YOU'VE TURNED TO THE DARK SIDE ... THAT YOU KILLED --
OBI-WAN WAS WITH YOU?
OBI-WAN IS TRYING TO TURN YOU AGAINST ME. I'VE BECOME MORE POWERFUL THAN ANY JEDI DREAMED OF, AND I'VE DONE IT FOR YOU. TO PROTECT YOU.
I DON'T WANT YOUR POWER OR YOUR PROTECTION! ANAKIN, ALL I WANT IS YOUR LOVE.
LOVE WON'T SAVE YOU. ONLY MY NEW POWERS CAN DO THAT. I WON'T LOSE YOU THE WAY I LOST MY MOTHER!
WE DON'T HAVE TO HIDE ANY MORE. I HAVE BROUGHT PEACE TO THE REPUBLIC. I AM MORE POWERFUL THAN THE CHANCELLOR.
I CAN OVERTHROW HIM, AND TOGETHER YOU AND I CAN RULE THE GALAXY. MAKE THINGS THE WAY WE WANT THEM TO BE!

I DON'T BELIEVE WHAT I'M HEARING ... OBI-WAN WAS RIGHT...
I DON'T WANT TO HEAR ANY MORE ABOUT OBI-WAN!
THE JEDI TURNED AGAINST ME...
...THE REPUBLIC TURNED AGAINST ME.
DON'T YOU TURN AGAINST ME!
ANAKIN, I'LL NEVER STOP LOVING YOU, BUT YOU ARE GOING DOWN A PATH I CANNOT FOLLOW.
I DON'T KNOW YOU ANYMORE...
BECAUSE OF OBI-WAN?
YOU'RE WITH HIM. YOU'VE BETRAYED ME!
NO, ANAKIN... I SWEAR...
LET HER GO, ANAKIN!

WHAT HAVE YOU AND SHE BEEN UP TO?!
LET HER GO!
YOU WILL NOT TAKE HER FROM ME!
UNNH!
YOU TURNED HER AGAINST ME!
YOU DID THAT YOURSELF.
YOU'VE LET THE DARK LORD TWIST YOUR POINT OF VIEW UNTIL YOU'VE BECOME THE VERY THING YOU SWORE TO DESTROY!
DON'T LECTURE ME, OBI-WAN. I SEE THROUGH THE LIES OF THE JEDI. I DO NOT FEAR THE DARK SIDE AS YOU DO.
I HAVE BROUGHT PEACE AND SECURITY TO MY NEW EMPIRE...
YOUR NEW EMPIRE?! MY ALLEGIANCE IS TO THE REPUBLIC, ANAKIN...
IF YOU ARE NOT WITH ME --
-- THEN YOU ARE MY ENEMY!

CORUSCANT...
YOU WILL NOT STOP ME! DARTH VADER WILL BECOME MORE POWERFUL THAN EITHER OF US!
FAITH IN YOUR NEW APPRENTICE, MISPLACED MAY BE...
...AS IS YOUR FAITH IN THE DARK SIDE OF THE FORCE!
DESTROY YOU, I WILL --
-- JUST AS YOUR APPRENTICE, MASTER KENOBI WILL DESTROY!

BLAAT!
I AM BEING CAREFUL! I'VE GOT A GOOD HOLD ON HER, BUT...
...I'M WORRIED ABOUT MY BACK. I HOPE IT'S ABLE TO HOLD UP UNDER THIS WEIGHT.
DON'T MAKE ME DESTROY YOU, MASTER!
YOU'RE NO MATCH FOR THE DARK SIDE!
I'VE HEARD THAT BEFORE, ANAKIN -- BUT I NEVER THOUGHT I'D HEAR IT FROM YOU.
THE FLAW OF POWER IS ARROGANCE!
YOU HESITATE -- THE FLAW OF COMPASSION!

THERE IS NO SIGN OF HIS BODY, SIR.
THEN HE IS NOT DEAD. HE IS HIDING SOME-PLACE...
DOUBLE YOUR SEARCH.
TELL CAPTAIN KAGI TO PREPARE MY SHUTTLE FOR IMMEDIATE TAKEOFF --
"-- I SENSE LORD VADER IS IN DANGER."
FAILED, I HAVE.

GAAAAAHH!
OBI-WAN!
YOU WERE THE CHOSEN ONE. IT WAS SAID YOU WOULD DESTROY THE SITH, NOT JOIN THEM!
YOU WERE MY BROTHER, ANAKIN.
I LOVE YOU...
...BUT I WON'T HELP YOU.
I HATE YOU!

SHORTLY...
THERE'S SOMETHING OUT THERE.
HE'S STILL ALIVE. GET A MEDICAL CAPSULE, IMMEDIATELY!
THE REMOTE ASTEROID STATION OF POLIS MASSA...
FAILED TO STOP THE SITH LORD, I HAVE. STILL MUCH TO LEARN, THERE IS...
ETERNAL LIFE...
THE ABILITY TO DEFY DEATH CAN BE ACHIEVED, BUT ONLY FOR ONESELF. A SHAMAN OF THE WHILLS DISCOVERED THE SECRET --
-- BUT IT WILL NEVER BE ACCOMPLISHED BY A SITH LORD. IT IS A STATE ACQUIRED THROUGH COMPASSION, NOT GREED.
WITH MY HELP YOU WILL BE ABLE TO MERGE WITH THE FORCE AT WILL.
A GREAT JEDI MASTER YOU HAVE BECOME, QUI-GON JINN. YOUR APPRENTICE I GRATEFULLY BECOME.
OBI-WAN HAS MADE CONTACT. HE HAS PADMÉ WITH HIM!

TWINS?!
SAVE THEM WE MUST. OUR LAST HOPE, ARE THEY.

DON'T GIVE UP, PADMÉ.
IS IT A GIRL?
LEIA.

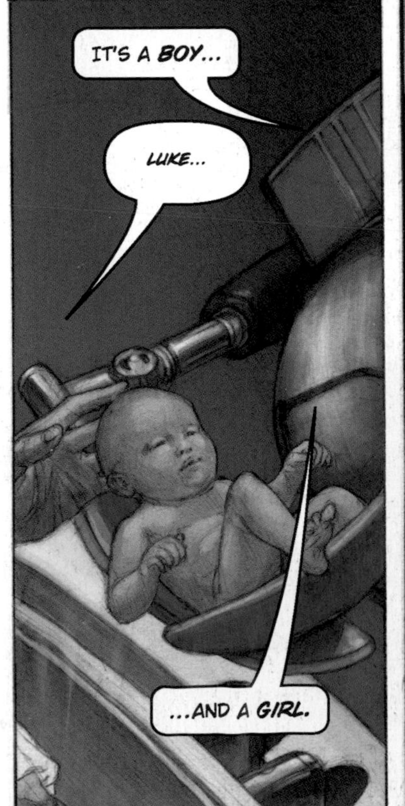
IT'S A BOY...
LUKE...
...AND A GIRL.

YOUR TWINS NEED YOU, PADMÉ. HANG ON...
OBI-WAN, THERE... IS GOOD IN HIM. I KNOW THERE IS...

TO NABOO, SEND HER BODY. PREGNANT, SHE MUST STILL APPEAR. HIDDEN, SAFE, THE CHILDREN MUST BE KEPT.
SPLIT UP, THEY SHOULD BE.
WE MUST TAKE THEM SOMEPLACE WHERE THE SITH WILL NOT SENSE THEIR PRESENCE.
MY WIFE AND I WILL TAKE THE GIRL. SHE WILL BE LOVED WITH US.
AND WHAT ABOUT THE BOY?
TO TATOOINE. TO HIS FAMILY, SEND HIM.
I WILL TAKE THE CHILD AND WATCH OVER HIM.
MASTER YODA, DO YOU THINK ANAKIN'S TWINS WILL BE ABLE TO DEFEAT DARTH SIDIOUS?
STRONG THE FORCE RUNS, IN THE SKYWALKER LINE. ONLY HOPE, WE CAN.
UNTIL THE TIME IS RIGHT, DISAPPEAR, WE WILL.
IN YOUR SOLITUDE ON TATOOINE, TRAINING I HAVE FOR YOU.
AN OLD FRIEND HAS LEARNED THE PATH TO IMMORTALITY. ONE WHO HAS RETURNED FROM THE NETHERWORLD OF THE FORCE TO TRAIN ME --
-- YOUR OLD MASTER, QUI-GON JINN. HOW TO COMMUNE WITH HIM, I WILL TEACH YOU.
QUI-GON?! I WILL BE ABLE TO TALK WITH HIM?
HOW TO JOIN THE FORCE, HE WILL TRAIN YOU.

CAPTAIN ANTILLES. I'M PLACING THESE DROIDS IN YOUR CARE. TREAT THEM WELL.
YES, YOUR HIGHNESS.
CLEAN THEM UP AND HAVE THE PROTOCOL DROID'S MEMORY WIPED.
OH, DEAR.
CORUSCANT.
MY LORD, THE CONSTRUCTION IS FINISHED. HE LIVES.
GOOD. GOOD!
LORD VADER, CAN YOU HEAR ME?
YES, MY MASTER.
WHERE IS PADMÉ? IS SHE ALL RIGHT?
I'M AFRAID SHE DIED.
IT SEEMS IN YOUR ANGER...
...YOU KILLED HER.

NOOOOOO!!!

DAGOBAH.
SPACE.
ALDERAAN.

TATOOINE.
THE END...
AND THE BEGINNING.